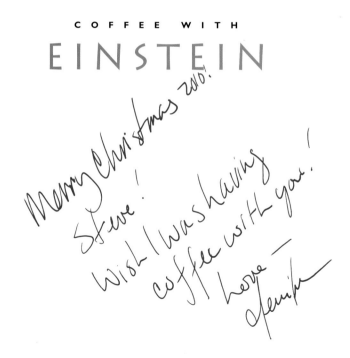

Merry Christmas 2010!

Steve!

Wish I was having

coffee with you!

love —

Jenifer

C O F F E E   W I T H

E I N S T E I N

CARLOS I. CALLE

FOREWORD BY SIR ROGER PENROSE

DUNCAN BAIRD PUBLISHERS

LONDON

Coffee with Einstein
Carlos I. Calle

To the memory of my parents, Martin and Lillian

Distributed in the USA and Canada by
Sterling Publishing Co., Inc.
387 Park Avenue South
New York, NY 10016-8810

This edition first published in the UK and USA in 2008 by
Duncan Baird Publishers Ltd
Sixth Floor, Castle House
75–76 Wells Street, London W1T 3QH

Managing Editors: Gill Paul and Peggy Vance
Co-ordinating Editor: James Hodgson
Editor: David Hibberd
Assistant Editor: Kirty Topiwala
Managing Designer: Clare Thorpe

Library of Congress Cataloging-in-Publication Data Available
ISBN-10: 1-84483-613-4   ISBN-13: 978-1-84483-613-0
10 9 8 7 6 5 4 3 2 1
Printed in China

For information about custom editions, special sales, premium and corporate
purchases, please contact Sterling Special Sales Department at 800-805-5489
or specialsales@sterlingpub.com.

Publisher's note:
The interviews in this book are purely fictional, while having a solid basis in biographical
fact. They take place between a fictionalized Albert Einstein and an imaginary interviewer.
This literary work has not been approved or endorsed by Albert Einstein's estate.

CONTENTS

Foreword by SIR ROGER PENROSE

The first third of the 20th century was quite extraordinary, in that our picture of the fundamental nature
of physical reality underwent *two* revolutions—and
Albert Einstein, who now sits opposite with cup of
coffee in hand, was a key figure in both.

One of these revolutions had to do with the very
peculiar character of the smallest constituents of
Nature. At the beginning of the century, in order
to explain the equilibrium states of matter and
light, Max Planck proposed that energy could be
transferred from one to the other only in little
discrete bundles. No one seemed to appreciate the
import of this until Einstein, five years later in 1905,
realized that light, which had seemed to have been
perfectly explained by Maxwell in the mid-19th
century, as interweaving waves of electricity and

magnetism, must now be simultaneously understood as made up, at its smallest scales, of little particles! Einstein's picture of light, regarded as mere fancy by most of his contemporaries, was strikingly confirmed by the initially sceptical American physicist Robert Millikan by 1916. This fundamental wave/particle paradox led eventually to the *quantum revolution*, finally formulated a decade or so later.

Einstein is much better known, however, for his *theory of relativity*, which radically changed our view of space and time, and then gravitation. Actually, this revolution came in two distinct stages. In 1905, Einstein put forward his *special* theory, reconciling the seemingly impossible requirements of a finite speed of light, as demanded by Maxwell's observationally well-confirmed theory, and a requirement that uniform motion should not be detectable by local measurement. Others before Einstein had been working towards his 1905 resolution of this conundrum, and had already found many essential ingredients, but Einstein's point of view was more far-reaching, and had one particularly noteworthy conclusion: the equivalence of mass and energy, as embodied in his famous $E=mc^2$. In 1908 the Russian Hermann Minkowski reformulated these ideas as four-dimensional *space-time*.

Remarkable though special relativity was, it was the natural conclusion of many independent investigations, both theoretical and experimental. Einstein's 1915 *general theory of relativity* was, however, a bolt from the blue. Einstein had had the extraordinary insight that by bringing in *gravity*, the relativity principle could be extended from uniform motion to arbitrary acceleration, and Einstein saw that this led to a picture in which Minkowski's space-time must be *curved*! Most physicists and astronomers found this hard to take, and confirming observations remained sparse during Einstein's lifetime. Einstein's general relativity is now well tested, and even serves as an invaluable probe for ascertaining mass distributions in distant reaches of the universe.

On the personal side, Einstein was effusive, and enjoyed a joke. He loved music, playing the violin, and also sailing. He felt strongly about politics, espousing pacifist views. In his later years, he cared little about his appearance, though photographs of him in earlier years tell a different story.

The world is enormously the richer for his having been here. Now let us meet him!

INTRODUCTION

Albert Einstein claimed to dislike giving interviews.
"To be called to account publicly for what others have
said in one's name, when one cannot defend oneself,
is indeed a sad predicament," he wrote in a short
essay. Fittingly, his formula for success in life was:
"If A is success, I should say the formula is $A=X+Y+Z$,
X being work and Y being play." "And what is Z?"
"Keeping your mouth shut."

However, Einstein failed to follow his own
formula. He gave countless interviews on a wide
variety of subjects—as a figure in the public eye, he
could not avoid this. However, he never sat down for
a comprehensive, structured interview that would
cover his entire scientific career, touching on the
most interesting aspects of his private life. That's the
intent of my posthumous "interview" over coffee.

What would be better than to have Einstein himself explain his theories to us? But can we understand relativity by reading an interview? Relativity is perceived as being one of the most esoteric theories, understood only by specialists. In fact, the main ideas of relativity are not difficult to grasp. Einstein said once that except for the mathematics all physical theories should be capable of being described in such a way that even a child can understand them.

Are the answers given in my "interview" really true to the essence of Einstein? For the most part, they are. I have drawn upon the views he expressed in his articles, books for the general reader, interviews with the press, and private letters to his family and friends. In some cases, I use direct quotes from these sources: these are identified in the Notes section at the back of the book.

Einstein's personal life is also an important component of these imaginary conversations. Was he an absentminded genius who worked endless hours in his study, emerging only after he'd made a discovery? At times, engrossed in his scientific endeavors, he appeared to fit the stereotype. Once, at a ceremony in his honor, he continued to scribble equations on the back of the program, oblivious to a speech that was praising his accomplishments. In fact, he was not really absentminded: he simply preferred work to pomp and ceremony.

However, it was not only work that drove him. We also read what Einstein had to say about his family, the women closest to him, his religious beliefs, and other facets of his rich and complex life. I selected these topics to be able to present as complete a picture of his life and his science as is practicable within the compass of this book.

ALBERT EINSTEIN (1879–1955)
His Life in Short

He had dashing good looks and piercing dark eyes, and he performed miracles. He turned ordinary fixed space into a twisted, curved space that shrinks or expands as you move, and ordinary time into an elastic, changing time that speeds up or slows down depending on your own motion. He created a universe using equations that flowed from his mind onto a sheet of paper, and the real universe turned out to be just like his equations told him it should be. With his mind alone, he changed our conception of the world forever.

The genius that Albert Einstein was to be is not revealed in his upbringing. He was born to Jewish parents on March 14, 1879 in the city of Ulm, in southern Germany. A year after his birth, his family moved to Munich, where he lived until he was fifteen. When he was two, his sister Maja was born and the family of four led a pleasant middle-class life.

Einstein's parents thought that he was a slow developer, and before he was three they took him to see a doctor because he had not yet learned to speak. We have no record of what the doctor said, but Einstein eventually learned to speak like any other normal child. Einstein himself would later say that this delay was due to his decision to speak only in whole sentences. He would first compose a sentence in his mind, and when he thought it was acceptable, he would say it: that way, no one would think that he could not speak properly.

Einstein's mother Pauline instilled in her children a love of music and made sure that they both learned to play an instrument. When Einstein was six, he started violin lessons, and although the lessons stopped when he was fourteen, love of the violin remained with him throughout his life.

Einstein's school record is spotty. He excelled in his elementary education, consistently earning top marks at a good school, even though he had skipped first grade. However, when he reached secondary school, he became selective about what he studied, and as a result he did very well in mathematics and Latin, subjects he liked, but performed poorly in Greek, a class he detested. His Greek teacher told him that he would never amount to anything!

Einstein disliked the rigid, militaristic school system but enjoyed learning on his own. When he was about twelve, he began tackling the problems in a geometry textbook. In a few months, he had not only completed them all but had even developed his own proofs for some of the theorems. Einstein said that this "holy geometry book" was what started his interest in science. At about the same time, he pleasantly surprised his engineer uncle, who had given him an algebra book, by finding solutions to even the most difficult problems.

Einstein continued with this program of self-study, teaching himself differential and integral calculus and analytical geometry by the age of sixteen. Meanwhile, his dislike of regular school continued, and when his parents had to move to Italy for financial reasons, Einstein dropped out of school, joining his parents a few months later. His parents' disappointment subsided when he promised to study for the college entrance examination on his own.

When Einstein thought he was ready, he applied to take the admission examination for the Zurich Polytechnic Institute, only to find out he was too young. After his mother convinced the university administration that her son was gifted, he was allowed to sit for the test. He failed. Although he excelled in math and science, he did poorly in just about everything else. At the suggestion of the Institute's director, Einstein enrolled in a Swiss secondary school for a year: a diploma from this school would guarantee admission to the Polytechnic.

The Swiss school offered a relaxed learning environment that encouraged students to think for themselves—unlike the German schools that Einstein disliked so much. The school's director was a respected teacher and scholar. He had three daughters, and one of them, Marie Winteler, became Einstein's first love. He was in heaven. To cap that wonderful year, Einstein obtained the necessary diploma with the top grades in the class.

Einstein entered the Zurich Polytechnic Institute in the fall of 1896 to study physics, although he was still under the minimum required age for admission.

There, he studied with world-class professors in state-of-the-art laboratories. As in secondary school, Einstein eagerly attended the classes he liked and skipped the ones he did not like, preferring to learn on his own. He excelled in the intermediate examinations at the end of the second year, finishing first in the class.

Einstein lost interest in Marie soon after starting college. During his second year, he met Mileva Maric, a physics student from Serbia. They soon fell in love and spent most of their free time together, often reading and discussing physics books.

The most exciting discovery in physics at the time was James Clerk Maxwell's theory of electromagnetism, the successful union of electricity and magnetism that explained the way that light moves through space. Einstein was extremely disappointed that the professor teaching the course in electricity and magnetism did not cover this. He not only made it clear that he disliked the course's approach but also became argumentative and disrespectful in this and other classes.

After graduating from the Polytechnic in 1900, Einstein wanted to study for a doctorate in physics, but the professors he had antagonized prevented him from doing so. He became, instead, an examiner at the Swiss Patent Office in Bern.

Einstein's new job isolated him from the scientific work of the universities and he was thus free to pursue his own scientific interests without the influence of peers or current fads. As before, he worked on his own, this time toward his doctorate.

During this period, Einstein's relationship with Mileva became serious, leading to their marriage in 1903. A year earlier Mileva had given birth to their daughter Lieserl. The couple kept this out-of-wedlock pregnancy secret and it seems that the daughter was given up for adoption. Her existence was discovered only in 1987 among Einstein and Mileva's letters to each other.

In 1904, when Einstein was about to storm the scientific world with his discoveries, his first son, Hans Albert, was born. With his mind mainly on his physics, Einstein failed to pay much attention to either wife or son, and the marriage began to sour.

The couple's second son, Eduard, was born in 1908 and the marriage improved for a couple of years. However, Einstein did not help matters by flirting with women during his now frequent trips to conferences and lectures. One in particular, his cousin Elsa Löwenthal, was especially close. When Einstein moved his family to Berlin, where Elsa lived, to accept an attractive offer from the university, Mileva became jealous and the marital problems grew worse. The couple finally separated in 1914 and divorced in 1919. Although Einstein had not yet won a Nobel Prize, he offered to give Mileva its proceeds if ever he did. He received the Physics Prize in 1921 for his work leading to the development of quantum theory.

In 1905, the 26-year-old Einstein published five scientific papers that changed the world of science forever. Three, in particular, prompted the two revolutions that shaped modern physics into the form we know it today. One was the paper that started quantum theory, the physics of atoms and molecules. The other two were on the theory of relativity, the theory that changed our conception of space and time. The second of these was the $E=mc^2$ paper, the famous equation that eventually explained how the sun burns its fuel and made possible nuclear energy and the nuclear bomb. However, in 1905, nuclear physics did not exist, much less the concepts of chain reaction and nuclear fission, both of which are essential for the bomb. Einstein came up with the equation in his effort to discover the workings of the universe: "Not a hint of possible technological applications was in sight," he wrote in 1955.

The goal of the two remaining papers of that miraculous year was "to find the facts which would guarantee as much as possible the existence of atoms of definite finite size," as Einstein put it. The first of these papers, "A new determination of molecular dimensions," was Einstein's doctoral dissertation, accepted by the University of Zurich in 1906.

Soon after his successful publication of the theory of relativity, Einstein began to see its limitations and started to look into expanding it. The effort turned out to be very difficult, even for Einstein, but after a decade in development he published the new theory in 1915. The general theory of relativity, as Einstein called it, describes the physics that governs the mechanics of the universe and extends and corrects Newton's own masterpiece, his theory of gravity.

Like his first ("special") theory of relativity, the general theory of relativity made strange predictions. Strangest perhaps was that space is not flat: planets, stars, galaxies, in fact all objects, warp the space around them, although this warping is measurable only near massive objects like a star or the sun. When British astronomers confirmed this phenomenon in 1919, Einstein was catapulted to worldwide fame. "Revolution in Science. New Theory of the Universe. Newtonian Ideas Overthrown," was the headline in the London *Times*. Other major newspapers around the world followed suit. Einstein became a celebrity.

The scientist capped this triumphant year by marrying his cousin Elsa Löwenthal five years after the breakup of his marriage to Mileva. Einstein had met Elsa when they were growing up but lost contact with her by the time he entered college. They reacquainted themselves during one of Einstein's visits to his mother in Berlin in 1912 when he was 33. The visit started a relationship that reached beyond family affection. Einstein's enthusiasm for Elsa lasted only two years but she never gave up and had an opportunity to win back her cousin's heart by caring for him when he fell ill with a chronic stomach ailment in 1917. Although by now Einstein's passion for Elsa had faded, he felt comfortable in her care and loved her cooking. He also felt a dutiful need to repay her devotion to him. Elsa, in turn, accepted that life with Einstein was not going to be easy. The prize was her role as Einstein's wife, sharing in the limelight of her famous cousin. It was a marriage of convenience for both of them.

In 1919, when the bending-of-light prediction of general relativity had been confirmed, World War I had just ended. Einstein had been against the war, a lonely pacifist in the midst of the general euphoria of the initial victories, declaring that "at such a time as this, one realizes what a sorry species of animal one belongs to. I doze quietly with my musings and only experience a mixture of pity and revulsion." In the 1920s, after his universal recognition, Einstein traveled around the world giving lectures and meeting with scientists and dignitaries. He used his newfound fame to speak for peace. During one interview, Einstein said: "I would unconditionally refuse to do war service, directly or indirectly, and would try to persuade my friends to take the same stand, regardless of the cause of the war."

Hitler's rise to power in 1933 changed these views. Einstein became alarmed and frustrated that the powerful nations of the world were not doing anything to prevent the danger of the Nazi threat. He decided to speak out against the Nazis, thus becoming one of their prime targets. Fearing for his life, Einstein moved to the United States, accepting an offer to lecture at the Institute for Advanced Studies in Princeton, where he remained for the rest of his life.

In 1939, he agreed to write a letter to President Roosevelt appealing to him to ensure that the US develop a nuclear bomb ahead of the Nazis. After the war, Einstein returned to his strong pacifist views, speaking against proliferation of nuclear weapons, a stance that earned him a 1,427-page FBI file.

Soon after completing his general theory of relativity, Einstein decided to apply its equations to build a model of the universe, in an attempt to discover how it was made and how it works.

The equations for the model gave him a dynamic universe, one that was either expanding or contracting. Because astronomers' observations showed that the universe apparently did neither, he introduced a factor—the *cosmological constant*, he called it—to make his model static.

A few years later, the astronomer Edwin Hubble discovered that the universe was not static after all but was expanding. Einstein realized that if he had stuck to what his equations were telling him, he would have predicted the expansion. He called the introduction of the cosmological constant his "greatest blunder." (However, observations made in recent years suggest that the cosmological constant that Einstein introduced in his equations might actually be correct. This constant, now called dark energy, is a repulsive gravitational force that explains why the expansion of the universe is accelerating, despite the fact that the universe contains enough matter to slow down this expansion.)

Einstein firmly believed that nature could be understood "through something basically simple and unified." After he completed his general theory of relativity, he dedicated the rest of his life to an unfinished search for a unified field theory, a single theory including all the interactions and fields in the universe.

Einstein's guide in his discoveries had always been simplification through unification—finding the common thread, the *symmetry*, in apparently very different concepts, like space and time, energy and mass, or acceleration and gravity. Uncovering these symmetries led him to his special and general theories of relativity. He was also led by his search for symmetry in his efforts to unify the whole of physics. Today, over half a century later, the search for symmetry is guiding fresh attempts at unification that may one day achieve Einstein's dream.

Einstein enjoyed his work and life in Princeton: "I am privileged by fate to live here in Princeton as if on an island," he wrote in March of 1936 to his friend Queen Elizabeth of Belgium. "Into this small university town … the chaotic voices of human strife barely penetrate." Sadly, the serenity of his sanctuary was shaken a few months later by the death of his second wife Elsa, his guardian angel for two decades.

However, he soon adjusted to life without Elsa. His dear sister Maja, his trusted secretary Helen Dukas, and his stepdaughter Margot took over and managed Einstein's household to near perfection. Not his appearance, however. A neighbor, Pam Harlow, remembered seeing the famous scientist stepping out of the house on his way to the Institute in his rumpled old clothes and his unruly hair, not worrying about avoiding a dip in the flagstone that would fill with water when it rained. Harlow, who was eight at the time, lived with her parents across the street from Einstein: "He never wore socks, not even in the winter," she said. "He would walk right into the wet puddle, and water would pour all inside his shoes."

Einstein was never too concerned with comfort or with material possessions. His sister Maja said that even in his youth he would say, "All I'll want in my dining room is a pine table, a bench, and a few chairs." His mind was always occupied with fundamental, not with material things. He wanted to know how the universe was made and how it worked, if the universe had to be constructed in the way it is, and whether it had to exist at all. He searched intensely for the answers to these questions until the last few hours of his life.

NOW LET'S START
TALKING ...

Over the following pages, Albert Einstein engages in
an imaginary conversation covering fifteen themes,
responding freely to searching questions.

The questions are in red italic type;
Einstein's answers are in black type.

COUNTING ATOMS

Einstein's first original contributions to science started right after he graduated from college. At the time, thanks largely to the work of the English chemist and physicist John Dalton (1766–1844), the existence of atoms was generally accepted, although a few scientists still resisted believing that they were real. All scientists did agree that atoms, if they existed, were too small to be seen. It was not until the 1950s, with the invention of the field ion microscope, that atoms became visible. In his early papers of 1902 through 1904, Einstein laid the foundation for his discovery of the facts that led to the unequivocal proof of the existence of atoms.

Professor, I'd like to discuss your first discoveries. What was the nature of your first published scientific papers?

My first two papers are not worth discussing. The first of any value, albeit small, are three papers published between 1902 and 1904, which allowed me to develop the ideas that would establish without any uncertainty the existence of atoms. These ideas came to maturity in 1905.

We learn in school that John Dalton had introduced his atomic theory around the beginning of the 19th century. Was the existence of atoms still in doubt in 1905?

There were still a small number of prominent scientists who didn't accept the need for them. Not only had Dalton introduced his atomic theory, but other scientists had shown how interactions between

molecules, which are made of combinations of
atoms, could successfully explain the transformation
of substances. Yet renowned scientists like
Ernst Mach and others denied the existence of
atoms. It's an interesting example of how even
brilliant scientists with a superb intellect can be
prevented from accepting the facts by holding on
to preconceived ideas.

How did you prove the existence of atoms?

I used an indirect method. Atoms are too small to
see with the naked eye and even the best electron
microscopes allow you to see objects only as small as
a millionth of a millimeter, or about 3,000 atoms.
Although at the time no one knew these dimensions,
I did know that atoms had to be detected indirectly.
While having tea at a friend's house one day, I began

to think about the motion of the sugar molecules dissolved in the water and figured out a way of calculating the sizes of those molecules.

Can you describe your method?

The method is based on the fact that when sugar is added to the water, its viscosity increases—that is, the water becomes denser, heavier. This viscosity is a quantity you can measure. I wanted to see if I could obtain a mathematical relationship between the size of the molecules and this measurable viscosity, from which I might deduce the size of the molecules. I had to make some assumptions about the molecules in order to get to this relationship.

By assumptions, you mean trying to guess what these molecules are like?

No, I couldn't guess that. My assumptions were about the shape and behavior of the molecules. I was actually trying to simplify the problem, to make it manageable so that I could perform the calculations. The sugar molecules in my calculation were perfect spheres moving around in the water unaffected by the presence of the others. I knew that actual molecules couldn't be perfect spheres, but for my calculation, that detail wasn't important. It wouldn't affect the results.

Was the relationship that you obtained very complicated?

The calculation was a two-step process involving two quite simple equations. The method was novel: I first obtained an expression in terms of the size of the sugar molecules and Avogadro's number. Avogadro's number is a critical quantity because with it you can calculate the number of molecules within a defined mass of any substance.

Professor, I'm going to need some help understanding Avogadro's number.

Avogadro's number is a fixed number that's connected to the properties of atoms. It's very useful because it allows you to count by weighing. For example, if you know that a dozen oranges weigh two kilograms, you can determine the number of oranges in a large shipping crate by weighing the crate. If you find that the oranges in the crate weigh two thousand kilograms, you know you have a thousand dozen oranges. This is faster and easier than counting twelve thousand oranges. If you needed to count dust particles, you wouldn't start by weighing a dozen minute particles. You'd need to start with a million, perhaps. Avogadro's number is much larger than a million because it's needed to count molecules which are ten thousand times smaller than dust particles. Instead of weighing a dozen or a million molecules, you weigh Avogadro's number of molecules. But before you're able to do that you need to know Avogadro's number very well, and determining a number with 24 digits isn't easy. As a result, previous attempts weren't very accurate.

So, with your method, you not only found the value of the size of a water molecule but a more accurate value of Avogadro's number as well.

That's correct.

And measuring the sizes of molecules and Avogadro's number proved that atoms exist.

These measurements led to the proof. I found several other methods to measure molecular sizes and Avogadro's number. It was the extraordinary agreement among all the independent methods to measure these quantities that convinced the few remaining diehards of the existence of atoms and molecules.

What were some of the other methods you found?

The most important were perhaps the ones described in my papers on Brownian motion. In 1828, the botanist Robert Brown observed with a microscope that pollen grains floating in water experienced a jittery motion. I didn't know about Brown's work until I was ready to write my paper, so I came to it from a different perspective. I knew that molecules at room temperature had significantly large energies and I asked myself whether those energies were large enough to move small particles of matter that could be seen under a microscope. That would work as a kind of molecular microscope, a method to visualize the invisible molecular motion by observing instead the motion of the much larger pollen grains. The motion of a grain due to the collision of one single molecule can't be measured, but during many random collisions sometimes a grain is hit multiple times on one side and the resulting motion can be observed.

If I follow you correctly, the molecules collide with the pollen particles and push them around in all directions. The jittery motion of the particles magnifies the molecular motion.

That's correct. To show that these microscopically visible particles moved because of molecular collisions, I made similar assumptions as with my earlier paper. I obtained an equation for the time between collisions, the distance traveled by the specks, the viscosity, and the particle radius. It was easy for an experimenter to use a stopwatch and a microscope to measure these quantities and find Avogadro's number. In a way, you could now count atoms.

Did it take long for someone to verify your results?

No. Within three years of the publication of my main papers on Brownian motion in 1905, Professor Jean Perrin in Paris confirmed all aspects of my theory.

THE YEAR OF WONDERS

In a now famous letter, Albert Einstein gave
his friend Conrad Habicht a preview of what
would become known as his year of wonders,
1905—comparable in its importance only
to Newton's great year of wonders, 1666: "I
promise you four papers … the first of which
I might send you soon. The paper deals with
radiation and the energetic properties of light
and is very revolutionary, as you will see."
That year Einstein in fact produced five papers
that turned the scientific world upside down
and started two major revolutions in physics.
Among them were his two beautiful papers on
the theory of relativity and a third that gave
birth to quantum physics.

Professor Einstein, most people associate your name with the theory of relativity and with the famous equation $E = mc^2$. When did those discoveries come about?

In 1905, while I was working as a clerk in the Bern patent office. However, these discoveries didn't happen suddenly. I was directed toward them in steps that arose from the laws of physics, which in turn were derived from observation.

But the actual discoveries were made that year, is that right, Professor?

Yes. It was a very productive year for me because I was able to find solutions to many of the things with which I had been struggling. I wrote my first five papers of any importance during that year and they dealt with the most important unresolved problems in physics at the time. The first dealt with radiation and the energy properties of light and the second with a method to measure the sizes of atoms, as we've already discussed. With my third paper, I was able to show that atomic motion can be discovered by studying the motion of small particles of about one thousandth of a millimeter floating in a liquid. The fourth was my special theory of relativity. My final paper of that year was actually a corollary to my relativity paper—a short paper showing that energy and mass are equivalent.

The last one is the $E=mc^2$ paper?

Yes, that's correct.

Would it be fair to say that most of your major discoveries were published in this year?

I would say that my major discoveries came to fruition then. However, that doesn't include my general theory of relativity, which came out much later, in 1915.

Did your paper on the energy properties of light lead to a new theory of light?

In a way, it did. It provided the foundation for quantum physics, which is the theory of matter and radiation. I was looking at an interesting new equation that Max Planck had developed to explain for the first time a vexing problem concerning the radiation of hot bodies. Planck's work was exciting because it solved that particular problem, but in an unorthodox way. It implied that this radiation was emitted or absorbed only in bundles or packets— what became known as *quanta* of radiation.

And that's the quantum in quantum physics?

Yes. But Planck didn't think his quanta were real: he believed that they were only mathematical artifacts used to make the equation work. I demonstrated that not just radiation from hot bodies but all radiation and light were actually made up of these individual quanta. Fifteen years later, other physicists developed quantum physics from these ideas.

Professor, you referred to one of your papers of 1905 as being on the special theory of relativity. Was this the famous paper where you first published your great discovery?

Yes. I wrote it soon after I finally understood the connection between space, time, and the speed of light.

I don't pretend that I'd be able to understand relativity in such a short time, but could you perhaps give me at least an indication of what you did in this paper?

Briefly, relativity extended the work of Newton, and in doing so it changed his view of time and space. For Newton, time passes at the same rate for all observers, regardless of the way they move. Newtonian space is the stage upon which things happen, and it never changes. According to relativity, space and time aren't fixed, they change when observers move, while the speed of light stays the same. It's the constancy of the speed of light that causes time and space to change. It's in this sense that time and space are relative.

I may be able to see how the flow of time may change, but I don't see how space can change when I move.

You may be confusing the physical flow of time with the psychological passage of time that we all experience. Relativity requires that actual physical time and space change as the observer moves, but this motion must be at speeds much greater than any human being has ever experienced. That's why these changes don't appear intuitive to us.

Your final paper was concerned with your $E=mc^2$ equation. You called it a consequence of relativity. How was this a follow-up and what does the equation mean?

I considered the relative motion of an atom emitting light and, by using the equations of relativity, showed that the mass of the atom decreased after the light emission. The $E=mc^2$ equation says that energy and mass are equivalent and that one can change into the other under certain circumstances.

Professor, you've whetted my appetite for your explanations of your theories. I'm beginning to get a glimpse of the implications of your astonishing discoveries that took place during a single year. I'd like to come back to these topics later on in our conversation.

It would be my pleasure to talk to you about these matters.

OF TIME AND SPACE:
THE THEORY OF RELATIVITY

Einstein's most celebrated discovery, the
Theory of Relativity, changed forever our
understanding of space and time. Published
during his year of wonders of 1905, it quickly
attracted the attention of the world's best-
known physicists. Later known as the Special
Theory of Relativity, it appears to contradict
our everyday experiences, and for many
years after its publication people found it
to be beyond comprehension. The British
scientist Arthur Eddington was once asked if
it was true that only two people in the world
besides Einstein understood the theory. "I am
wondering who the other one might be," was
his tongue-in-cheek reply.

Professor Einstein, how did you come to discover the theory of relativity?

It's difficult to know how one discovers something— the mind is motivated by various complexities with different weights. The special theory took final form in about five weeks in 1905, after ten years of trying to resolve a paradox that I encountered at the age of sixteen: what would an observer see if he pursued a beam of light with the same velocity as that of the light? The definitive answer to the question required two assumptions, which became the foundation of the special theory: the principle of relativity and the principle of the constant velocity of light.

I have the feeling that I'd need to understand these two principles if I hope to ever understand the theory of relativity. Could you, please, explain them?

I'll use an easy illustration. If I stand inside the sleeper cabin of a train traveling on very smooth tracks at a steady speed and drop a stone, I see the stone descend in a straight line. If the cabin has the curtains drawn closed so that I can't look outside, the motion of the stone won't reveal to me whether the train is moving relative to the Earth or is stationary. Moreover, no experiment I may attempt inside this cabin can ever allow me to discover the motion of the train. Everything behaves in the same way whether the train moves or remains at rest. The laws of physics are the same for all observers in steady motion or at rest. This is the principle of relativity.

And this is true for any speed of the train?

Yes, the principle of relativity applies to any state of motion as long as this motion is at a steady or constant speed, with no accelerations or turns. And a constant speed includes zero speed, or rest. Rest and motion depend on a reference point. You may think that you're at rest while sitting on that chair. A space traveler will see you spinning with the Earth at 1,500 kilometers per hour. Rest and motion are relative concepts and the laws of physics apply equally to them. Once I understood this, I was able to resolve my paradox, which leads us to the second principle.

I think I'm ready for this now.

The principle of the constant velocity of light was not an easy notion to formulate. Consider again the example of an observer riding alongside a beam of light. Such an observer should see the stationary front edge of the beam. However, a *stationary* light wave seems to be an impossibility on the basis of scientific experiments and well-established theory. Moreover, on the basis of my principle of relativity, all observers in constant motion or at rest should experience the same phenomena. According to this principle, then, all such observers should measure the same speed of light. That was the resolution of my paradox, for no observer could ever hope to see the front edge of a light beam. Regardless of how fast they move, all observers should see light traveling at the same speed as that measured by an observer who, relative to Earth, is at rest. This insight became known as the principle of the constant velocity of light.

That insight, as you call your great discovery, is perhaps one of the most difficult ideas for people to grasp.

That's because it's not an intuitive notion. What *is* intuitive is that if you are a passenger on a train, for example, and the train is moving at 40 kph and you're walking from the back to the front of a train car at 5 kph, someone outside the train would say that you're moving at 45 kph. But it seems different with light. If you shine a beam of light from the back of the moving train, the light, the photons that your lamp sends off, travels at a speed of about a billion kph, a speed that I call c. In this case, a pedestrian outside the train doesn't measure c plus 40 kph, but only c.

Why is it different with light? Why doesn't the pedestrian outside the train measure the speed of light to be c plus 40 kph in the same way that he measures the passenger's speed to be 40 plus 5 kph? I'm confused.

You should be confused. I was in conflict with this idea for a long time, because there's an apparent contradiction. The solution to this dilemma came

to me one night in 1905 after a long discussion with
my friend Michele Besso. That night I went home
still troubled by the problem, but the next morning
I had the solution and told Besso straight away. My
solution dealt with the concept of time. I realized that
time isn't absolute—it's connected to the velocity of
light. It was now clear in my mind—the speed of light
is fixed when you move, but time and space change.
Time is relative and space is relative. That's the
essence of the special theory of relativity.

*How do time and space change? That idea seems so
removed from everyday experience.*

In our everyday experience, everything moves at
comparatively small speeds and we don't notice
anything odd about space and time. In reality, the
pedestrian measuring the speed of the passenger

walking at 5 kph as the train travels at 40 kph doesn't measure 45 kph. If the pedestrian had access to extremely precise instruments, he would measure a slightly slower speed than 45 kph, about one ten-thousandth of a billionth of one percent less. The reason for the difference is that time slows down when you move, affecting the value of the speed you measure. Since we can't perceive that tiny difference, we don't notice and think that it's exactly 45 kph.

So, not everything is relative, as some people are fond of saying when referring to your theory. Time and space are relative but the speed of light is not relative, it's constant.

Exactly! Space and time change when you move. They are both linked to the speed of light and change in such a way as to keep this speed always constant. Before relativity we had Newton's theory. For Newton, space and time were fixed, but all speeds were relative. Relativity turned this around.

I can't really say that I now understand *the theory, but I think I have an appreciation of what it implies.*

Understanding comes initially from our perception of the world around us. Our senses aren't keen enough to experience relativistic effects without attaining the extremely large speeds required for their direct appreciation. Before we leave the topic, here's yet another application of the principle of relativity for your delight. Today I'm described in Germany as a "German savant," and in England as a "Swiss Jew." Should it be my fate to be represented as a *bête noire*, I should, on the contrary, become a "Swiss Jew" for the Germans and a "German savant" for the English.

ABOUT TIME

According to Einstein's special theory of relativity, time no longer flows at the same rate for everyone: it changes when you move. However, to be able to notice this change, you would have to be moving at close to the speed of light, and no vehicle comes even close to approaching these extremes. Subatomic particles do, however. Certain particles formed at an altitude of 10,000 meters last only a couple of microseconds—their short lives allow them to travel a mere 600 meters before disintegrating. Yet, they are found near the Earth's surface. The theory of relativity solved this paradox. From our reference point, time flows more slowly for these particles and, as a consequence, their lives are extended.

Professor Einstein, I'd like to return to the idea that time and space change. I believe you said that time slows down when you move at great speeds. So if I move fast enough, my days would last longer.

Not according to *your* clock. However, if *I* look at your clock, I'd see that it has slowed down compared to the clock in my room. I must tell you that this effect is real, it's not just something in my imagination nor in yours. Now, we've all experienced that when we're happy and content, time *seems* to pass more slowly. That's a psychological phenomenon, not a physical one. The relativistic change in the flow of time is a physical phenomenon that can and has been measured.

Would it be possible to understand this effect without complex mathematics or even without any math at all?

We can try a *thought experiment*, an experiment that we can carry out in our minds, but making sure we obey the laws of physics. And it won't require any math. Imagine that you're on a super-fast train that can travel at speeds close to the speed of light. If the train moves at a constant speed, everything inside it behaves in the same way as when the train is at rest.

That's your principle of relativity, correct? You can't distinguish rest from steady motion.

That's right. Uniform motion can't be detected. Let's continue with our thought experiment. At some point during the night, while the train travels at a relativistic speed, a flashbulb located exactly in the middle of your car is fired. You'll then see the light from the flashbulb reaching the front and back of the car at the same time.

Yes, that's clear, Professor. Because the flash is in the middle of the train, the light from the flashbulb travels the same distance in both directions and reaches the two ends at the same time.

Now, try to imagine that I'm standing outside looking at your relativistic train with a telescope. Through a window in your train car, I observe the light traveling away from the flashbulb. Since the train is moving, I see that the back end of the car moves closer to the place where the flashbulb was when it fired. As a result, the light has a shorter distance to travel than the light traveling to the front of the car, which has actually moved farther away.

It appears that we perceive the same phenomenon differently. Is this the case?

Yes, but the important thing to understand is that two events that happened simultaneously for you—the arrival of the light at the front and back of your train car—were seen by me as not happening at the same time.

Is that what you mean when you say that time is relative?

Yes, but it's more than that. Let me walk you through a simple illustration. Imagine the flashbulb in the train car was actually hanging from the ceiling and I placed a light sensor on the floor of the car, right under the flash, so that when the light from the flashbulb reaches the sensor, it causes it to fire the flash again. If it did that repeatedly, you can see that I could use this setup as a clock—the ticking of your clock is the firing of the flash.

You'd want both observers to measure their own time by counting these cycles, right?

Correct. For you, observing on the train, you simply see the light from the flashbulb on the ceiling traveling straight down to reach the sensor. The length of the path that the light travels is the height of the ceiling. However, I see that by the time the light reaches the sensor, the sensor would have traveled some distance forward. The path of the light that I see is longer than the one you see, so for me the clock takes longer to tick. Notice that we only have one clock, but you see it ticking faster. Time flows faster for you when you move relative to me.

And you say that this is a real phenomenon. It isn't just your particular clock?

It isn't just the clock. Your heart beats more slowly, your metabolic processes take longer, and you age at a slower rate.

It's a kind of time machine. All I have to do is get on a fast spaceship for some time and I'll return younger.

When you return, your relatives and friends would have aged faster. Yes, you could think of it as a time machine into the future.

MASTERPIECE

The special theory of relativity only applies
to motion at a constant speed along a straight
line (what Galileo called *uniform motion*).
Soon after the publication of the special theory,
Einstein started to try and extend it so that it
would include all types of motion, uniform
and accelerated. His efforts came to fruition
in 1915, after a decade of extremely hard work.
Along the way, he had to learn new mathematics,
enlisting the help of Marcel Grossmann, one
of his college friends—now a professor of
mathematics—for that part of the endeavor.
The result was the general theory of relativity,
which scientists have called the greatest
scientific theory ever developed. It is
considered to be Einstein's masterpiece.

Professor Einstein, what would you regard as your greatest achievement?

My general theory of relativity, the generalization of the special theory to include all motion. It is a system of the world.

In what way is it a generalization of the special theory?

When you consider the special theory, you see that it aims at areas beyond its domain. Why should the laws of nature remain unchanged only for the case of uniform motion? The laws of the universe should be fully independent of the type of motion. After I developed the special theory, I set out to do just that—generalize it so that it would include accelerated motion.

Why wasn't accelerated motion in the special theory?

The special theory is based on the principle that uniform motion is undetectable—you can't become aware of it unless you refer to an outside reference point. You can, on the other hand, detect accelerated motion. For example, you know right away when your train is starting to move, takes a turn, or stops without having to look outside for a reference point. Thus, accelerated motion is not relative and can't be included in the special theory. Generalizing the theory to include it turned out to be extremely difficult. I didn't know where to start.

I can begin to see the difficulty. Accelerated motion needs to be included in relativity, but since it isn't relative, it can't be. How did you finally resolve this impasse?

I had to look for another property that would remain undetectable under certain conditions.

I had a great motivation to do so because the extension of relativity to include accelerated motion would automatically include gravitation, since motion under gravity is an accelerated motion. In 1907, while preparing a comprehensive paper on the special theory, it suddenly occurred to me that a person falling from the roof of a house wouldn't feel his own weight—that is, he wouldn't feel gravity. That was the most fortunate thought of my life—it made me realize that gravity is also relative and that it depends on the state of motion of the observer. This thought propelled me toward the general theory.

I see how gravity could be considered relative, since it exists for someone on the ground but not for someone falling toward the ground, as you've explained. Is gravity the property that remains undetectable?

Not just gravity but acceleration in general. I'll give you an example. A group of scientists are working in a windowless laboratory aboard a spaceship that's continuously accelerating at one g. In this ship, the scientists aren't weightless because they feel pushed to the floor with the same force as the gravitational force back on Earth. If one of the scientists lets go of one or two objects, these float in space until they collide with the floor of the lab, which is accelerating in their direction. From the frame of reference of the scientists, who are moving with the ship, these bodies are accelerating to the floor of the lab exactly at one g, as if the lab were on the ground on Earth. It's impossible for the scientists to determine experimentally if they are still accelerating at one g or back on the ground on Earth. The laws of physics are the same in both instances. Acceleration and the effects of gravity are the same phenomenon.

Couldn't you distinguish acceleration if the ship were
accelerating at one-third g, for example? You'd know
that you weren't on the ground on Earth, right?

Yes, but you couldn't distinguish that acceleration
from the effects of Martian gravity, which has the
value of one-third g. The acceleration due to gravity
depends on the mass of the celestial body you are
close to.

I see now, Professor. It's not terrestrial gravity that's
important, but the acceleration due to gravity near
any celestial body.

Yes, any value of the acceleration of the ship would be
indistinguishable from the gravitational acceleration
to a certain body. This insight put me on the path
toward general relativity. But the path was thornier

than expected, since it required one to move away from Euclidean geometry, where space is flat, to a new geometry where space is curved. The curvature of space implies that light is propagated curvilinearly in a gravitational field. To be able to observe this phenomenon, one needs a strong gravitational field, like the field generated by the Sun. Even so, its detection requires very precise instrumentation.

How did the curvature of space come about in the theory?

The equivalence between gravity and acceleration can take you to it. Returning to the laboratory aboard the accelerating spaceship, one can see that if the scientists examine the path of a ray of light coming horizontally through a small hole on one side of the ship, they see a curved path. I'll sketch it for you on the back of this envelope:

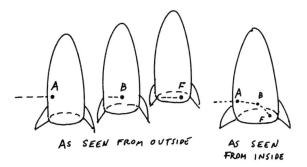

AS SEEN FROM OUTSIDE

AS SEEN FROM INSIDE

It might help you visualize it if you think of a small meteorite that penetrates the accelerating ship. When the meteorite first enters through the hole A, the ship is at a certain position. An instant later, when the meteorite has moved a small distance to B, the ship has accelerated away from this location but the meteorite continues moving along its original path. From the perspective of the meteorite, the ship accelerates in its direction and the floor of the laboratory moves to meet it. From the perspective of the scientists standing on that floor, the path of the meteorite bends and hits the floor here at point F. The same is true for a ray of light: the scientists will see the path of the light ray bending and striking the floor. Since acceleration is the same as gravity, we conclude that a gravitational field also curves the path of a ray of light. That result was of great importance because it could be compared with reality.

Your sketch does help me to understand it. So the bending-of-light prediction was confirmed?

Yes, that prediction was confirmed by the British astronomical expedition of 1919. This measurement isn't easy to make, since the curvature of space close to the gravitational field of the Earth is extremely small. But the Sun's gravitational field causes a curvature that, in principle, could be measured.

I'd calculated the small deviation of light rays from a star passing the Sun at a grazing angle. The star's light could be seen during a solar eclipse and that's why Arthur Eddington traveled to West Africa to measure it during the solar eclipse of 1919. He obtained exactly the amount I'd calculated.

Your discovery showed how the laws of nature are designed. What would you have said if the results had been different and the theory proven wrong?

Then, I would have been sorry for the dear Lord. The theory is correct.

QUANTUM THEORY AND REALITY

Einstein's first paper of his year of wonders marks the beginning of the long road toward the full development of quantum theory completed by Niels Bohr (1885–1962), Werner Heisenberg (1901–1976), Erwin Schrödinger (1887–1961), and Paul Dirac (1902–1984) in the early 1920s. Einstein never fully accepted quantum physics, because it is a theory of probabilities, not certainties, and he felt it would one day be superseded. Today, several experiments have shown that quantum theory does describe correctly the way nature is. However, there are problems integrating quantum physics with general relativity; and either theory, or both, may one day be supplanted by a more complete theory that integrates them.

Professor Einstein, you said earlier that your first paper of 1905 provided the foundation for quantum physics. What is quantum physics?

Quantum physics governs the behavior of atoms, molecules, subatomic particles, and light. It's the physics of the very small. In contrast, general relativity is the physics of the very large, from rocks to planets and galaxies. Quantum physics was developed out of the need to explain several important observations of the behavior of matter and radiation that couldn't be explained with Newtonian physics. The fundamental reason for the failure of Newtonian mechanics in the realm of the atom is that the world turned out to be grainy, not continuous. When you consider radiation, for example, you find that it is made up of very small packets or quanta of energy which are indivisible. It's similar for matter:

when atoms or molecules interact and absorb or give off energy, they do so by means of quanta of energy. An atom can't absorb half a quantum of energy, since such a thing doesn't exist. Newtonian physics expects the world to be continuous and that's why it fails at the atomic level.

So, both quantum physics and relativity showed Newtonian physics to be incorrect.

No. Newtonian physics was shown to be *incomplete*, not incorrect. It is still correct for objects much larger than atoms moving at speeds not close to the speed of light. In fact, both quantum physics and relativity become Newtonian physics for those sizes and velocities. However, no theory is ever proven to be completely correct. It is entirely possible that general relativity could one day be shown to be incomplete—the theory that may replace it should encompass it and expand it, keeping the same approach. However, I think that quantum physics, in spite of its success, isn't the right approach.

If quantum physics is not the right approach, is there a theory that can replace it?

There isn't any other theory now that can replace it, and I believe it will take a long time to develop one. I must tell you that I'm in the minority in regarding quantum physics to be incomplete. Great physicists like Bohr, Heisenberg, Dirac, Born, and many others disagreed with me on this. When pressed, Bohr would say that even if quantum physics were one day replaced by a more comprehensive theory, this new theory would still have the probabilistic properties of quantum physics. I disagree.

If I follow what you're saying, it's the probabilistic properties of quantum physics that you object to. What are those properties specifically?

Quantum physics does not provide a mathematical representation of the atom or its structure, or of any other physical entity that exists in space and time. What quantum physics does is to determine the *probability* of finding these particles at a specific location, or in a specific state of motion, when a measurement is performed. I have no objections to the logical construct of the theory and I recognize its important successes. However, the theory forbids one from knowing at once everything one wants to know about an object. One may not ask both where an electron is and how fast it's moving *at a given time*. One can't even ask *what* an electron is. In quantum physics, those questions have no meaning. But one can calculate the probability of finding the electron at a given location if one attempts to measure it. If quantum physics is correct, one can never know for certain the past or present, much less calculate the future of anything in the universe. I cannot accept that. The theory gives us much, but I don't think that it really uncovers God's secrets. I, at any rate, am convinced that God is not playing dice. I believe that quantum physics provides only a temporary interpretation of the world. I think that one day a model of reality will be developed that will represent the objects themselves and not the probability of their existence.

THE EQUATION

Einstein discovered his famous $E=mc^2$ equation
a few months after completing his paper on the
special theory of relativity. In a magnificent
three-page paper—the last paper of his year
of wonders—he showed how the equations of
relativity implied that energy has mass. Some
time later, he was also able to show that mass
has energy. "This result is of extraordinary
importance," he wrote then. But was the
equation correct? Einstein had some doubts,
and a few weeks after publication he wrote in a
letter to his close friend Conrad Habicht: "the
line of thought is amusing and fascinating, but
I cannot know whether the dear Lord doesn't
laugh about this and has played a trick on me."

Professor, I'd like to turn now to your famous $E = mc^2$
equation. You said earlier that the equation states that
energy and mass are equivalent and that one can change
into the other. Could you give an example of this?

The equation says that the mass of an object is a
form of energy and that energy is a form of mass.
A pair of common magnets can easily illustrate this.
If, while holding the magnets, you allow them to
come together with the north pole of one magnet
facing the south pole of the other, the magnets will
pull your hands together. The energy required to
pull your hands comes from the conversion of part
of the mass of the two magnets into energy. If you
had an exceptionally precise scale, you'd find that
the two magnets weigh slightly less when they
are together than when they are apart. The actual
value can be calculated with the $E = mc^2$ equation.

The energy E given off, which is contained in the magnets, is equal to the decrease in mass (m) times the speed of light (c) squared. Since the speed of light is such a large number, about 300,000 kilometers per second, the minuscule mass loss of the magnets yields a sizable amount of energy.

If matter contains so much energy, why did this phenomenon remain unnoticed?

The mechanisms needed to release large energies, like the ones seen in nuclear reactions, hadn't been discovered. Unless sufficient energy is given off, it can't be measured. It's like the case of a very wealthy man who never spends much of his fortune— no one would know he was wealthy. The equation had to be deduced theoretically using the theory of relativity.

In what way did your $E=mc^2$ equation make the atom bomb possible?

The equation was one of many theoretical and experimental discoveries made in our search for the nature of the universe that were used in the construction of the bomb. During radioactive disintegration, when an atom splits into two atoms, a relatively large amount of energy is released. The equation itself says nothing about how to bring about such a split. To illustrate the radioactive disintegration process, we can use the example of our wealthy man again. The original atom that splits into two fragments is like the rich man who has a large amount of money hidden away. When he dies, he leaves all his money to his two children under the condition that they donate a small fraction of their inheritance to the community. The children together end up with less money than their father had, but the man was so wealthy that this small donated fraction is still a large amount of money that destabilizes the local economy.

Without the equation, the bomb wouldn't have been possible.

Yes, but you also need quantum mechanics and nuclear physics, which were developed after the equation.

Professor, does the equation have other applications?

The discoveries in nuclear medicine are a direct application. The equation also explains how the millions of tons of hydrogen that are squeezed together in the core of the Sun each second convert some of their mass into the energy that makes life on Earth possible.

THE BOMB

"Sir: Some recent work … leads me to expect that the element uranium may be turned into a new and important source of energy in the immediate future." These were the opening words of a letter that Einstein sent to President Roosevelt in 1939 urging him to develop a nuclear bomb ahead of Nazi Germany. Although ultimately other political events led to the start of the Manhattan Project to develop the first nuclear weapon, Einstein deeply regretted the letter. He was a pacifist before the Nazi threat, but became a "militant pacifist" during World War II, serving as a consultant for the US navy on a variety of issues related to weapon design and explosive capabilities. He returned to his stronger pacifist views after the war.

Professor Einstein, if you'd known how the atomic bomb would be used, would you still have written that now-famous letter to President Roosevelt?

That is a painful question for me. I now believe that I made a great mistake in writing that letter. There was, of course, justification for writing it: the fear that the Nazis would develop the bomb first. The threat of Hitler was so horrifying that I abandoned my absolute pacifism.

When and how was the letter written?

In July of 1939, the physicist Leo Szilárd came to my house in Princeton with the alarming news of Germany's imminent invasion of Belgium, a country with a large stockpile of uranium. We knew by then that uranium was fissionable and that, given time and funding, a powerful nuclear bomb could be made. Originally, Szilárd had wanted me to write to my friend Queen Elizabeth of Belgium. Knowing of the grave danger, I agreed straight away and in a few days I gave a draft of this letter to Szilárd. He came back later with the physicist Edward Teller and gave me a new draft that he'd written, now addressed to President Roosevelt. I didn't like Szilárd's draft and decided to dictate another draft to Teller. Szilárd later wrote two versions of this letter and sent them to me for approval. I signed them both. The longer version was delivered to the President in October.

You weren't part of the Manhattan Project that built the bomb. Were you asked to participate?

My involvement in making the bomb ended with the letter to the President. Instead of prompt action, my letter resulted in the formation of a committee to study the issue. I was asked by the President to serve on that committee but I declined. I was not asked to participate in the Manhattan Project when it was established right after Pearl Harbor. I would have refused that invitation, too, if it had come.

You said earlier that you had to overcome your pacifist views because of the Nazi threat. Did you return to those views after War World II?

Yes. My pacifist feeling wasn't acquired intellectually but is instinctive and innate. I believe that the killing of human beings in a war is no better than common murder. Before War World II, I'd strongly stated my refusal to do war service in any form and said that I'd attempt to convince my friends to take the same position, regardless of the war. I believed then that if only two percent of those called to war declared themselves conscientious objectors, and at the same time demanded that all conflicts be resolved peacefully, wars would end. That was, of course, years before Hitler appeared on the scene. If I'd known that the Nazis weren't going to succeed in making the bomb, I would never have signed the letter to the President. After the war, I very soon returned to my pacifist views and have often spoken against the proliferation of nuclear weapons. I'm a *dedicated* but not an *absolute* pacifist—this means that I am opposed to the use of force under any circumstances except when confronted by an enemy who pursues the destruction of life as an *end in itself*.

Once we learned to make nuclear weapons, there was no turning back—the genie was out of the bottle. How do we stop other countries from acquiring the bomb?

That's probably impossible. What must change
are the policies of the powerful nations. We came
out of a world war in which we were forced to endure
the shameful low ethical practices of the enemy.
The Nazis started the practice of bombing civilian
centers and the Japanese then did the same. The
Allies then had to respond in kind and even more
effectively. However, after the war, instead of
re-establishing the sanctity of human life and the
safety of innocent civilians, we continue degrading
to the same low standards in our present conflicts.
This policy only creates antagonism and enhances
the danger of war. I don't know how the Third
World War will be fought, but I can tell you what
they will use in the Fourth—rocks!

*Is it justifiable for any country to possess nuclear
weapons?*

The United States and the other industrialized nations that now possess the bomb have agreed to use it only as a deterrent. I believe that this is the correct policy. To possess the bomb without the promise of not using it unilaterally is a misuse of the bomb for political ends, with the sole purpose of creating fear in the enemy.

Do you think that humanity will be able to survive this atomic age?

The discovery of atomic power doesn't have to bring about the destruction of the world any more than the discovery of fire. If we do everything in our power to prevent the misuse and proliferation of atomic weapons, humanity will survive. But if every effort fails and men end up destroying themselves, the universe will not shed a single tear for them.

UNFINISHED BUSINESS

"After an unremitting search during the past two years I now believe I have found the true solution," wrote Einstein in 1925, referring to his new unified field theory, a single theory encompassing all the forces of nature. His enthusiastic statement turned out to be too optimistic and he would later admit that, on more careful consideration, the true solution was not at hand. Einstein spent the last 30 years of his life working relentlessly on this quest for unification. On Sunday, April 17, 1955, feeling slightly better after having suffered an aneurysm the previous Wednesday, he asked for his notebook and continued with his calculations. He died a few hours later, at one o'clock on Monday morning.

Professor Einstein, is there a discovery you would have liked to have made, a Grail that slipped your grasp?

My search for the unification of all fields, a single theory that could describe the nature of the universe, has been my lifelong goal. I'm convinced that this unification will be achieved one day because I cannot accept the idea that nature works through separate fields that have no connection with each other. Electromagnetism, gravity, and matter should come naturally out of this unified field theory.

I'm afraid I don't fully understand the significance of this unification. Why would the fields need to be unified? Why couldn't nature have different fields?

Each individual field theory is incomplete by itself. Moreover, the individual theories of physics contain subtle inconsistencies. Historically, whenever separate theories have been brought together, the inconsistencies have been resolved. Reformulating Maxwell's electromagnetism in the light of the principle of relativity removed the inconsistent view of absolute motion that it had with Newton's mechanics. Quantum physics and general relativity offer inconsistent views on reality. Both cannot be correct, and a theory that unifies them should resolve the inconsistency. I believe that the distinct fields we have today are a manifestation of a single, consistent unified field that I'd like to discover.

So then we'd know how everything in nature works.

Not in every single detail, but in very general terms, yes. We'd know why gravity is what it is, we'd see where all the properties of the electron and the proton come from and why they attract or repel each other. We'd understand all the interactions in nature and see how they make possible all that we observe in the world.

Could you give me an idea of your approach?

My broad idea was to extend general relativity so that it would encompass all other fields, thus creating a theory of pure geometry that would include all matter. Material particles like electrons would be small distortions of space and time, much like wrinkles in a piece of fabric. The theory would solve the problem of understanding how an electron can be a point particle with no extension in space, as quantum theory requires. When I developed my first unified theory with this approach, I discovered that it had a feature that I'd failed to understand at the time:

it predicted the existence of mirror-image particles to the electron and the proton. Dirac predicted these mirror-image particles a few years later using a different approach. They were discovered some time later and are known today as antimatter. Not understanding this feature in my theory was one of my great blunders.

Was that first approach of yours correct, then?

No. Even though it correctly predicted the existence of antimatter, it didn't predict the masses and charges of the electron and the proton and had to be discarded. Years later, after many other discarded attempts, I returned to this first attempt and expanded it. I've continued to work on it since. As a result, my first attempt is also my last, though it's not yet complete.

Do you think that this new theory, when completed, will be the one?

I believe so, but my colleagues disagree. In comparison to the recent developments in physics, my efforts seem old-fashioned since they don't include the quantum constant. But when the current statistical fad in physics passes and we return to the deterministic view, which I believe is correct, this theory will be the starting point for the full unification of physics. What really interests me is whether God could have made the world differently— in other words, whether the demand for logical simplicity leaves any freedom at all. However, it may be that I'm on the wrong track. Who knows, perhaps He is a little mischievous.

THINKING WITH IMAGES

One of Einstein's collaborators, the physicist
Banesh Hoffmann, described what it was like
to work with Einstein. He and Leopold Infeld
worked with the great man in 1937, when he
was attempting to extend his theory of general
relativity to include electromagnetism. In his
authoritative biography, Hoffmann wrote that
when they encountered an obstacle in their
research, Einstein would simply stand up and
declare that he was going to do a little thinking.
He would then pace around the room for several
minutes, twisting a lock of his abundant hair
around his finger. Suddenly his face would light
up and, smiling, he would proceed to show them
the solution. What was the process that took
place deep in Einstein's brain?

*Professor Einstein, as a theoretical physicist all your
extraordinary contributions to science were achieved by
thinking. Are you aware of the way you think? Was there
something special taking place in your brain that made
these discoveries possible?*

That's impossible to answer, but the question has
intrigued me for some time and for this reason I'll
try to explain, with the obvious caveat that neither
I nor anyone else will ever know whether the answer
is correct. The way I think is the result of the specific
development of my mind's focus—from temporary,
personal matters to the mental grasp of nature.

In your case, was this development guided or accidental?

I suspect it was an interplay between what my
environment provided and how I wanted to proceed.

One is born with certain abilities, the environment provides input, and one makes choices.

And, in your case, this guided development led to a unique way of thinking?

It led to *my* way of thinking.

What is your way of thinking, if I may ask?

I tend to think in terms of *memory pictures*: images that form in the mind in response to sensual stimuli. However, I don't really believe that the formation of such images can yet be called *thinking*—not even when the formation of an image calls another, and this one calls a third in a series. Real thinking only takes place when the recurrence of these images in diverse circumstances develops into a *concept*—the generalization of diverse images into an abstract idea. A child forms the concept of "liquid" when he experiences a variety of substances that can be spilled or drunk. One must again be careful, since not all concepts can be formed as a result of images. *Truth*, for instance, won't match my description. A concept like that arises in our minds only when we agree to a convention regarding the rules of the game.

What do you think is the role of language in the formulation of thoughts?

I don't think it's necessary for a concept to be expressed in words. It's obvious that when that happens, the thought is communicable. However, it's clear to me that thinking takes place without the use of words. If this weren't the case, the spontaneous feeling of *wonder* that we all experience from time to time would not happen. We wonder when we experience something that conflicts with our accepted body of concepts. If the conflict is strong enough, it may affect our world of concepts, eventually becoming part of it. In this way, our thought world grows, as an incessant escape from wonder. I experienced this kind of wonder when I was a child of four or five years. My father gave me a magnetic compass and I was fascinated by the behavior of the needle. This behavior didn't fit into my world of concepts. My eventual resolution of this conflict helped to develop my world of concepts.

When during the different stages of development of your theories did images start to play a significant role?

During the early stages. The development of the special theory of relativity, for example, started with my attempting to visualize what would happen if I were to pursue a beam of light with the same velocity as the light. I should be able to observe the light oscillations at rest in front of me. As I studied Maxwell's electromagnetism, which governs the behavior of light, I learned that physics doesn't allow for such a stationary beam. A conflict formed in my mind. Its resolution came ten years later with my development of the special theory.

So, in the case of the compass, the conflict was added to your world of thoughts once you learned about magnetism. But in the case of the light beam, the explanation didn't exist and you had to develop it. Your resolution of this conflict produced the theory of relativity. Have I captured your thoughts correctly?

Yes. That's a good summary.

RELIGIOUS BELIEFS

Albert Einstein said that he was a deeply religious man. However, he had an unorthodox religious worldview, which he expressed in several essays about the relationship between religion and science. He also discussed his religious beliefs in letters to his friends and to a few admirers who wrote him requesting his opinions on God, prayer, and religion. Einstein's peculiar and sometimes colorful responses are often quoted out of context. In the case of his frequent references to God, these statements have been sometimes misinterpreted in support of one religious view or another. Einstein, however, was emphatic and clear about what he believed in and who his God was.

Professor Einstein, in several instances during our
conversation, you have mentioned God as the creator
of the universe. Do you believe in God?

I believe in a God who reveals himself in the orderly
harmony of what exists, not in a God who concerns
himself with the fates and actions of human beings.
I believe that the laws of nature manifest the existence
of a spirit vastly superior to Man and one in the face
of which we, with our modest powers, must feel
humble. I don't believe in a personal God, one that
rewards or punishes us for our good or bad deeds.
I think that this idea is naïve.

This superior spirit is the creator of the universe, then?

Yes. A vastly superior spirit created the universe
and its laws. Through my work, I am satisfied with

getting a glimpse of the wonderful and mysterious architecture of His world.

But if you don't believe in a personal God, I would assume that you're not a religious person.

On the contrary: I am deeply religious. But I don't belong to nor do I believe in any organized religion and I don't believe in the immortality of human beings. My religion consists of being aware of the existence of the most magnificent harmony and beauty in nature. For me, being religious is feeling a deep emotion in the discovery of the mysteries of nature and in the profound admiration of the creator of the universe. It's very different from the indoctrination practiced by the organized religions of the world. Indoctrination is the opposite of what being religious means to me.

Why do you consider the notion of a personal God to be naïve?

It's a primitive idea. It's the first stage in the human development of religion and develops to placate the fears faced by primitive societies: fear of hunger, sickness, wild animals, and death. A more advanced but still primitive stage results from our desire for love and nurture with a God that rewards and punishes. That's where the ideas of heaven and hell originate. A God that punishes evil and rewards good is an anthropomorphic God, with human qualities. I consider these ideas to be primitive and naïve.

How would you respond to people who claim that you're an atheist because you don't believe in a personal God, or to those who claim that you're actually a pantheist because your God is really nature?

I'm neither. I believe that there is a single creator of the universe. My belief is derived from the same discovery that a child makes when encountering a large library for the first time. The child marvels at the wealth of information in all of those books, and even though he's not able to understand all of what the books say, he knows that someone must have written them. A similar feeling comes to even the most learned and intelligent people when they discover the unity and order of the laws of nature. Although they may not understand these laws, they know that someone must have created them. Reverence and admiration for the creator of this marvelous harmony constitute what I call *cosmic religion*, which is the most advanced stage in the development of a religious feeling.

Do you think that religion and science are compatible?

Dogmatic, organized religion, with a God that intervenes in the events of nature is, in my opinion, in conflict with the rationality of science. Science has no use for this primitive religion of fear. However, cosmic religion, the religious feeling without a dogma and without a God with human qualities, is not in conflict with science. I believe that cosmic religion and science complement each other. Moreover, I think it's most important for scientists and for artists to awaken in themselves this cosmic religious feeling and to keep it alive. Indeed, I maintain that the cosmic religious feeling is the strongest and noblest motive for scientific research.

FATHER AND SONS

Einstein and his first wife Mileva had three children: a daughter whom they named Lieserl, who was born before they were married, and two boys, Hans Albert and Eduard. Hans Albert became a college professor at Berkeley. Eduard, a gifted boy, developed schizophrenia and, at the age of 23, was interned in a psychiatric hospital for the rest of his life. The fate of Lieserl is unknown: it is likely that she was adopted. Einstein was a loving but busy father who worked even while he was at home. After Einstein and Mileva separated in 1914, his relationship with his boys went through cycles of strain and affection.

Professor, we've discussed your work and your views on war and the nuclear bomb. At this point, I'd like to move to another aspect of your life. Would you be so kind as to give us some insights into your personal life?

With me, every peep becomes a trumpet solo. I'm convinced that there's too large a disparity between what I am and what people think I am. However, I understand to some extent the widespread interest in the lives of people like me who have had the misfortune of being in the public eye. For this reason, I'll agree to answer your questions, though not without some uneasiness.

I understand, and I thank you, Professor. I'd like to ask you about your children. Did any of them follow in your footsteps?

No. None of my children became physicists, but
Hans Albert was an accomplished professor of
hydraulic engineering at Berkeley. He had a good
mind and he would have made a good physicist,
but parents don't choose their children's careers.

What did your other children do?

Eduard had serious health problems that prevented
his full development. He had a superior mind and
learned to read on his own very early in life. He was
already multiplying and dividing numbers by the
age of five. His mental problems robbed him of a
brilliant career in medicine or science.

*With your extremely busy life, it must have been difficult
for you to achieve a balance between your work and your
family life.*

Yes. That's been a most regrettable consequence of my scientific career. Hans Albert was born shortly before I began all my work of 1905—that was the year of his first birthday. On one occasion my wife scolded me when she found me rocking little Albert on my knee while I made some calculations in a notebook. I don't think the boy minded.

Did your children get special instruction in mathematics from you? Did you help them with their homework?

Even though I wanted very much to be able to teach mathematics to Albert, living apart from him made it impossible. He took a liking to geometry, as I had done when I was his age, and that pleased me no end. His mother was able to coach him, assigning him problems. As for helping with their homework, the boys were bright enough to manage on their own.

*You mentioned that your son Hans Albert became a
professor, like yourself. Were you very close to him?*

Our tranquil moments together were few and far
between. During my years in Berlin, we had the
opportunity to get together for hikes or to go sailing,
activities we both enjoyed. When he was grown up,
the war and our occupations conspired to keep us
apart. I longed to spend time together with him but
such moments rarely came. I consoled myself with
the joy of having had a son who inherited the chief
trait of my personality: the ability to rise above mere
existence by sacrificing oneself through the years
for an impersonal goal.

EINSTEIN'S WOMEN

When Einstein's sister Maja was born, little Albert, then two years old, thought that the baby was a new toy and asked his mother where the wheels were. Maja died of arteriosclerosis of the brain in 1951 in her brother's house in Princeton where she'd moved in 1939, two years after she immigrated to the United States fleeing the Nazis. Einstein was not visibly moved by the death of loved ones, but after Maja passed away, he told a friend that he missed her more than he had ever imagined he would.

Einstein was married twice, first to Mileva Maric, a melancholic and somewhat troubled fellow physicist from Serbia who was Einstein's classmate in Zurich, and later, during his forties, to his first cousin Elsa Löwenthal.

Professor, did you have any siblings?

I had one, my dear sister Maja.

Were you close to her?

Yes, we were very close. We grew up together
in Munich and enjoyed each other's company
throughout our lives. She lived with us in Princeton
during her last twelve years. I read to her every
evening during her worsening illness, as her mind
remained clear for a long time. I had to endure her
death stoically, since my distant God makes these
events more difficult. She'd been my confidante
during the university years when I was courting my
first wife Mileva, when my parents vehemently, and
to some extent correctly, opposed that relationship.
My mother had a particularly difficult time with it.

Was your mother very strict when you were growing up?

She wasn't extraordinarily strict, but she was very
involved in our education. Her greatest gift to her
children was music, and it's because of her that I've
been able to appreciate it. She always supported
me in anything I did, with the sole exception of my
relationship with Mileva. Mileva was an intelligent
companion—I spent countless hours with her
studying and discussing physics. Our married life
was happy for a few years, but things deteriorated for
us, in large part owing to my work. We parted ways
when our children were still small, which affected
their lives. Perhaps a man of my type shouldn't marry
and have children.

Since we're talking about some of the women who were
important to you, are there others you'd like to mention?

My second wife Elsa was one of the most important people in my life. She was a tireless nurturer who nursed me through several illnesses. She ran our household with perfect efficiency, while her careless husband was preoccupied only with work. When we traveled together, I became a piece of furniture that she constantly arranged, in a futile effort to improve something about me. After she died, I became a kind of ancient figure known primarily for his non-use of socks, wheeled out on special occasions as a curiosity. I must also mention my secretary Helen Dukas and my stepdaughter Margot. Together with Elsa, they made possible my stubborn pursuit of the unified field theory without having to worry about mundane affairs. And, finally, there were the young women of my youth—I have to acknowledge them, though without naming them, for the happy hours in their company, playing music and enjoying life.

ON THE SHOULDERS OF GIANTS

As the most famous scientist of the 20th century,
Einstein was acquainted with all the renowned
scientists of his time and befriended many.
He had strong opinions on the major thinkers
who preceded him and, in general, spoke with
enthusiasm when he talked about them. Four
scientists were at the top of Einstein's list
of great men. In his study in Berlin, he had
portraits of three of them: Sir Isaac Newton
(1642–1727), James Clerk Maxwell (1831–1879),
and Michael Faraday (1791–1867). These
scientists along with Galileo (1564–1642)
were, in Einstein's view, the greatest creative
geniuses humankind ever produced, and he
freely acknowledged the debts he owed to them
in making his own discoveries.

Professor Einstein, Newton once said that his work rested on the shoulders of giants. Who were your giants?

Newton himself and Galileo. They created a complete system of the world based on a few laws. In comparison to Newton, what I was able to wrest from nature is insignificant. But the striving frees us from the bonds of the self and makes us comrades of those who are the best and the greatest.

What made the Newtonian system of the world the greatest scientific achievement?

Newton was the first person to discover a system based on experience, and from which one could obtain a wide range of phenomena by mathematical reasoning alone. His system explains the workings of the universe, from the motion of planets around the Sun to the motion of a pebble falling on a pond. This feat is nothing short of a miracle, and this miracle is due to the mind of Newton.

Others must have contributed. Galileo, for example?

Yes, they did—men like Kepler. But of Newton's predecessors, it's Galileo who towers above all others. His contributions reach almost as high as Newton's. Starting from experience and using an ingenious method to isolate the motion of an object, Galileo was able to show that in the absence of forces, this object will maintain its existing state of motion and that if the object does change its speed or direction, it must be because of an external force.

In everyday experience, you must apply a force to keep an object moving. Without the engine going, a car eventually

stops and a sailboat stalls with no breeze to push it.
Yet Galileo says that no force is needed to keep an
object moving?

That's Galileo's great achievement. He knew that
in everyday experience, friction, as an external
force, is always present. Lacking the technology
to remove friction in reality, Galileo did so in his
mind, thus isolating the moving object from all
external forces. The object's motion isn't disturbed
and the object remains moving forever. Newton
learned this from Galileo. Newton understood
immediately that these observations needed to
be interpreted mathematically. To do this he
invented calculus.

Was it the invention of calculus that made Newton
the greatest genius?

No, calculus was merely a new language that allowed him to formulate the laws of motion. His quantification of the concept of the application of external forces to change the state of motion of an object led to his discovery of the fundamental concept of mass. That was a greater achievement. But he didn't stop there. He used his new mathematical tool to demonstrate that the force that brings an apple down from a branch is the same force that keeps the moon in its orbit about the Earth. That was the astonishing leap that only the mind of Newton could have made. That achievement ranks as the greatest discovery in the history of humankind.

You've often mentioned your admiration for the work of James Clerk Maxwell. Do you regard him as close to the great Newton in the temple of science?

Not just Maxwell, but the twin geniuses Faraday and Maxwell. As a pair, I regard them as essentially equal to the Newton-Galileo pair in their contributions to science. Faraday extended the connection between electricity and magnetism that Ampère had discovered and invented the magnificent concept of fields of force. This was a new kind of physical reality that has been crucial for the development of present-day physics. The great Maxwell extended this work, gave it mathematical rigor, and produced the glorious theory of electromagnetism, teaching us among other things that electromagnetic fields spread as a wave with the speed of light. Maxwell discovered the nature of light!

You also mentioned Kepler. How influential was he?

Kepler provided the empirical mathematical laws

on the motions of the planets that made Newton's system of the world possible. Today, it's hard to fully appreciate the ingenuity and assiduous work required to discover the planetary laws. His good fortune was that precise data on the positions of Mars was available to him. However, to calculate the orbit, he needed two fixed points in space. One was provided by the Sun, but where was the other to be found? The planets are all moving around the Sun. Kepler realized that Mars traverses a given point in space once during each orbit. Since he had the data, he selected one of the locations in the orbit as his second fixed point. These two points in space made it possible to use triangulation to calculate the orbits of the Earth and the other planets.

We've talked about the giants who preceded you. Were there any giants during your own time?

Planck and the great Bohr, to be sure. Max Planck's law of radiation was the breakthrough that made possible the first exact determination of the correct sizes of atoms. More important, however, was his discovery of the atomistic structure of energy, a discovery that became the cornerstone of all of 20th-century physics. And Bohr constructed the first mathematical model of the atom and guided the modern interpretation of quantum theory, which gave us the most complete—and in my opinion, not yet final—theory of matter.

Did any non-scientists influence your work in any way?

No. I built my scientific work on the findings of the scientists we just discussed. But several thinkers influenced my life and helped shape my beliefs. The work of the philosopher Benedict de Spinoza helped shape my thinking on God and religion, and my discovery of Mozart's sonatas at a very early age triggered my lifelong love of music. The extraordinary lives of all these great men are a constant reminder that my inner and outer lives are based on the labors of other people, living and dead, and that I must exert myself in order to give in the same measure as I've received.

MUSICIAN AND SAILOR

Besides physics, Einstein passionately embraced two other activities throughout his life: music and sailing. He was a gifted musician and once stated that this was the only other profession he might have chosen. He revered the composers of the 18th century but had little interest in modern music or in the modern composers of his day, criticizing their "poverty of structure" and lack of "inner truth." He took to sailing with gusto, too, sailing often and dismissing the safety concerns of others, and never carrying life jackets, navigation charts, or a backup engine. "If I have to drown, then let it be honestly," he once said.

Professor Einstein, you've mentioned your love for music a couple of times. Is music important in your life?

Music is my passion. I can't conceive of living without being able to play music. Besides physics, music is what gives me most joy. I see my life in terms of music. My violin accompanies me wherever I travel.

When did you learn to play the violin?

My mother Pauline, who was an accomplished pianist, decided that my sister Maja and I should be exposed to music from an early age. She enrolled us both in music lessons. I was six then. That's when I chose the violin.

Most children don't enjoy their music lessons. Did you?

For the most part, I didn't. I disliked them very much, as I disliked any structured learning activity. I detested the antiquated mechanical methods used by the instructors, but when I was about thirteen, I discovered Mozart's sonatas, and my interest in music picked up. I wanted to be able to reproduce the unique and wonderful grace of Mozart's music. That's when my real learning started. Regrettably, my formal instruction continued only for about one more year. But, by attempting to play those beautiful sonatas, I was able to advance my technique. I believe I always learned anything better on my own.

Did your mother ever give you any music instruction?

Not really. However, after the lessons ended, I'd play duets with her, my mother on the piano and me on the violin. That became a tradition for us throughout her life. There was always a great deal of wonderful music playing in our home.

Did you play any other instrument?

I taught myself to play the piano. I was adequate at it. Playing the piano relaxes me. Often, when I come across some difficulty in my calculations, playing a few chords on the piano helps steer my mind toward a clear path. Music is magnificent for the mind.

Who were your favorite composers?

Certainly, Mozart and Bach—I listen to, play, love, and revere their music. I admire Beethoven, but I think he's too dramatic. I like Schubert because of his exceptional talent for expressing emotion. I also like the smaller works of Schumann because they are very original and have intense feeling. Brahms composed good chamber music, but most of his other works aren't convincing for me. I enjoy Vivaldi, Scarlatti, and Corelli. I play Mozart and Beethoven sonatas the most. This music always inspires me.

Is music your diversion from your work?

No, music is simply part of my life. When I play music I'm not working, but I don't play music to get away from my work. Music and research work are nourished by the same sort of longing, and they complement each other in the release they offer.

What activity do you pursue when you want to relax?

I've enjoyed sailing since my student days in Zurich. But I'm not so talented in this art, and I'm satisfied if I can manage to get myself off the sandbanks on which I from time to time become lodged.

Any memorable experiences from your sailing days?

Once, while attending a scientific conference in Geneva with Marie Curie, we found ourselves with some free time and I invited her to go sailing. When we were out in the middle of the lake, she said to me that she didn't know I was a good sailor. I replied, "Neither did I." Then she asked me what we'd do if the boat should overturn. "I can't swim," she said. "Neither can I," I replied.

Do you take your work with you when you go sailing?

I usually have a notebook with me for the occasions when there's no wind. I'm always striving to uncover the mysteries of nature, and feel that every minute I can spend on my work will bring me closer to discovering them.

Is your mind ever far from your science?

Not often. Music is perhaps the exception. I feel deeply the music I play or listen to. But seeking to discover nature's secrets is exhilarating, and this joyous activity constantly fills my mind. To be a scientist is to remain a child all through one's life, always marveling at the discovery of another wonderful phenomenon, always longing to eat at the Tree of Knowledge.

Your thoughts on this, Professor, lead me to my final question. Is science, with all its present shortcomings, on the right path to discovering nature's secrets?

Yes, I firmly believe that, in general, science is on the right path. But science is still in its infancy. One thing I've learned in a long life is that all our science, measured against reality, is primitive and childlike—and yet, it's the most precious thing we have.

NOTES

p.10 "To be called ..." *Ideas and Opinions* (New York: Crown Publishers, 1954), p.15.

p.10 "If A is ..." *The New York Times*, August 18, 1929. Quoted in A. Pais, *Einstein Lived Here* (New York and Oxford: Oxford University Press, 1994), p.152.

p.22 "Not a hint of ..." Letter to to Jules Isaac, Princeton, February 28, 1955. Quoted in A. Fölsing, *Einstein, A Biography* (New York and London: Viking, 1997), p.725.

p.22 "to find the facts ..." "Autobiographical Notes," in *Albert Einstein, Philosopher Scientist*, ed. P. A. Schilpp (London: Cambridge University Press; La Salle IL: Open Court, 1949), p.47.

p.25 "at such time ..." to Paul Ehrenfest, Berlin, August 19, 1914. *Einstein, A Biography*, p.343.

p.25 "I would ..." Interview with *Die Wahlheit* of Prague, 1929. Quoted in R.W. Clark, *Einstein, The Life and Times* (New York: World Publishing, 1971), p.351.

p.28 "through something basically simple ..." To Cornelius Lanczos, February 14, 1938. Quoted in H. Dukas and B. Hoffman, *Albert Einstein, The Human Side* (Princeton NJ: Princeton University Press, 1979), p.60.

p.29 "I am ... barely penetrate" To Queen Elizabeth of Belgium, March 20, 1936. Ibid., p.45.

p.30 "He never wore ... inside his shoes" Private conversation with Mrs. Harlow in McLean VA, November 11, 2006.

p.30 "All I'll want ..." Maria Winteler-Einstein, "Albert Einstein, A Biographical Sketch," in *The Collected Papers of Albert Einstein*, Vol. 1 (Princeton NJ: Princeton University Press, 1987), p.14.

p.42 "I promise ..." Letter to Conrad Habicht, May 1905. *The Collected Papers of Albert Einstein*, Vol. 5, Doc. 27 (Princeton NJ: Princeton University Press, 1995), p.31.

p.58 here's yet ... for the English.

Out of My Later Years (London: Greenwood Press, 1956; New York: Random House, 1970), p.57 (slightly adapted for the purposes of conversation).

p.75 Then, I would ... is correct. I. Rosenthal-Schneider, *Erinnerungen an Gespräche mit Einstein* manuscript, July 23, 1957; also I. Rosenthal-Schneider, *Begegnunger mit Einstein, von Laue, Planck* (Braunschweig, 1988). See *Einstein, A Biography*, p.439.

p.81 I, at any ... playing dice. Letter to Max Born, December 4, 1926. *The Born-Einstein Letters 1916–1955* (Basingstoke: Houndsmills; New York: Macmillan Press, 2005), p.88.

p.82 "This result ... importance," *Jahrbuch der Radioaktivität und Elektronik*, 4 (1907), p.442.

p.82 "the line ... trick on me." Letter to Conrad Habicht (Fall 1905, undated).

p.87 "Sir: Some recent ..." Letter to President Roosevelt, August 2, 1939, *The Albert Einstein Archives* (The Jewish National & University Library, The Hebrew University of Jerusalem, Israel), 33-143.

p.90 I believe ... murder. Letter to the editor of Japanese magazine *Kaizo*, September 22, 1952. Quoted in O. Nathan and H. Nordern, *Einstein on Peace*, pp.584–89 (*Einstein Archives*, 60-039).

p.91 I am a dedicated ... end in itself. Letter to Seiei Shinohara, June 23, 1953 (*Einstein Archives*, 61-297).

p.92 I do not ... —rocks! Interview with Alfred Warner, *Liberal Judaism* 16 (April–May, 1949), p.12, (*Einstein Archives*, 30-1104).

p.93 if every effort ... tear for them. Letter to Maurice Solovine, Princeton, May 7, 1952, in *Letters to Solovine* (New York: Philosophical Library, 1987), p.137.

p.94 "After an unremitting ..." Quoted in B. Hoffmann, *Albert Einstein, Creator and Rebel* (New York: The Viking Press, 1972), p.225.

p.99 What really interests ... freedom at all. Ernest Straus, in *Helle Zeit-Dunkle Zeit*, p.72. See *Albert Einstein, A Biography*, p.736.

p.99 Who knows ... mischievous.
Letter to Hermann Weyl. Quoted in
Einstein: The Life and Times, p.613.

**p.107 I believe in ... human
beings.** Reply to Rabbi Herbert
S. Goldstein, *The New York Times*,
April 25, 1929, p.60. Quoted in
M. Jammer, *Einstein and Religion*
(Princeton NJ: Princeton University
Press, 1999), p.48.

p.107 the laws of ... feel humble.
Letter to a young girl, January 24,
1936, reproduced in *Weltwoche*,
August 19, 1981, p.37. Quoted in
Einstein Lived Here, p.117.

**p.111 I maintain ... scientific
research.** "Religion and Science,"
The New York Times, November 9,
1930, pp.1–4. Reproduced in *Ideas
and Opinions* (New York: Crown
Publishers, 1954), p.39.

p.113 With me ... solo. To Paul
Ehrenfest, March 21, 1930. Quoted in
Albert Einstein, The Human Side, p.17.

p.116 who inherited ... goal.
Letter to Hans Albert Einstein, May
11, 1954 (*Einstein Archives*, 75-918.)

p.120 a kind ... curiosity. Letter
to Erich Mühsam, Princeton,

Spring 1942, in *Helle Zeit-Dunkle
Zeit*, p.50, see *Einstein, A Biography*,
p.732.

p.122 But the striving ... greatest.
Albert Einstein note to Dr. Hans
Mühsam, 1920, see *Albert Einstein,
The Human Side*, p.19.

p.129 my inner ... received. *Ideas
and Opinions* (New York: Crown
Publishers, 1954), p.9.

p.130 "If I have ..." *Einstein, A
Biography*, p.685.

p.131 I see ... music. Interview
with George Sylvester Viereck,
"What Life Means to Einstein,"
The Saturday Evening Post, October
26, 1929.

p.134 are ... offer. Letter to Paul
Plaut, October 23, 1928. (*Einstein
Archives*, 28-065); also in *Albert
Einstein, The Human Side*, p.78.

**pp.134–5 But I am not ... become
lodged.** Letter to Queen Elizabeth
of Belgium, March 20, 1954
(*Einstein Archives*, 32-385).

p.137 One thing ... we have. In a
letter to Hans Mühsam, July 9, 1951
(*Einstein Archives*, 38-408).

REFILL?

BOOKS

There is a substantial bibliography on Einstein's life and work. The books range from textbooks on his scientific work to biographies aimed at the general reader. In this list I have chosen the best books for general readers currently in print.

M. Born, *Einstein's Theory of Relativity* (New York: Dover Publications, 1962)

C.I. Calle, *Einstein for Dummies* (Hoboken: Wiley, 2005)

R.W. Clark, *Einstein, The Life and Times* (New York: The World Publishing Company, 1971)

H. Dukas and B. Hoffmann, *Albert Einstein, The Human Side* (Chichester, West Sussex and Princeton NJ: Princeton University Press, 1979)

A. Einstein, *The Collected Papers of Albert Einstein*, 10 vols. (Chichester, West Sussex and Princeton NJ: Princeton University Press, 1987–2006)

Autobiographical Notes (London and New York: Open Court, 1979)

Ideas and Opinions (New York and London: Crown Publishers, Random House, 1954)

Letters to Solovine (New York: Philosophical Library, 1987; London: Citadel Press, 1993)

Out of My Later Years (London and New York: Wings Books, Random House, 1956)

Relativity: The Special and the General Theory (London and New York: Penguin, 2006)

The Born-Einstein Letters (London and New York: Macmillan, 2005)

The World As I See It (New York: Citadel Press, 2007)

A. Einstein and L. Infeld, *The Evolution of Physics* (New York: Simon & Schuster, 1967)

A. Fölsing, *Albert Einstein, A Biography* (London and New York: Viking, 1997)

B. Hoffmann, *Albert Einstein, Creator and Rebel* (New York: Viking, 1972)

W. Isaacson, *Einstein: His Life and Universe* (London and New York: Simon and Schuster, 2007)

M. Jammer, *Einstein and Religion* (Chichester, West Sussex and Princeton NJ: Princeton University Press, 2002)

T. Levenson, *Einstein in Berlin* (London and New York: Bantam, 2003)

A. Pais, *"Subtle is the Lord ..." The Science and Life of Albert Einstein* (Oxford and New York: Oxford University Press, 1982)

Einstein Lived Here (Oxford: Clarendon Press, 1994)

J. Renn and R. Schulmann, *Albert Einstein-Mileva Maric, The Love Letters* (Oxford and Princeton NJ: Princeton University Press, 1992)

J. Stachel, *Einstein's Miraculous Year* (Chichester, West Sussex and Princeton NJ: Princeton University Press, 1998)

VIDEOS

Einstein's Big Idea, NOVA, PBS, Nova441 (2005)

Einstein Revealed, NOVA, PBS, Nova810 (2000)

Einstein's Wife, PBS, EINW601 (2003)

Einstein: How I See the World, PBS Home Video (2000)

Genius: The Science of Einstein, Newton, Darwin, and Galileo, NOVA, PBS (1974)

All available from http://www.shoppbs.org/

WEB RESOURCES

The Albert Einstein Archives, The Hebrew University of Jerusalem http://www.albert-einstein.org/

A list of other reputable sites is available online from http://www.aguidetophysics.com/EinsteinWebResources/, including links to documents, biographies, photographs, tutorials and courses, and radio and television broadcasts.

INDEX